Illustrated by Jerrod Maruyama

Customer Service: 1-877-277-9441 or customerservice@pikidsmedia.com

Published by Phoenix International Publications, Inc.
8501 West Higgins Road   59 Gloucester Place
Chicago, Illinois 60631   London W1U 8JJ

PI Kids and *we make books come alive* are trademarks of
Phoenix International Publications, Inc., and are registered
in the United States.

www.pikidsmedia.com

8 7 6 5 4 3 2 1

ISBN: 978-1-5037-5443-0

TINKER BELL'S
BEST BIRTHDAY PARTY

we make books come alive®

Phoenix International Publications, Inc.

Chicago • London • New York • Hamburg • Mexico City • Sydney

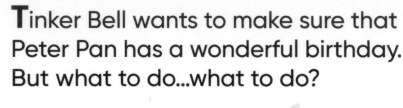

Tinker Bell wants to make sure that Peter Pan has a wonderful birthday. But what to do...what to do?

*Close your eyes for a
fantastic birthday surprise!*

"That's it!" says Tink. "I will throw a birthday party...a surprise party! I'll ask my Never Land friends to help!"

Shhh, quiet...it is a surprise for Peter!

Tinker Bell writes and sends beautiful invitations to all of Peter's friends. Then she calls everyone together to make a plan.

Shhh, quiet...it is a surprise for Peter!

"We'll get to work," say the Lost Boys. "We know a perfect place in the forest for the party."

Shhh, quiet...it is a surprise for Peter!

"We'll bring decorations!" say John and Michael. "Balloons and confetti will be great."

Shhh, quiet...it is a surprise for Peter!

"I can make a cake," Wendy says, "with candles on top! And we'll all sing 'Happy Birthday!'"

Shhh, quiet...it is a surprise for Peter!

"Let's disguise everyone as pirates!" says Mr. Smee, laughing. "I'll bring hats."

Shhh, quiet...it is a surprise for Peter!

"And we shall all play treasure hunt," says Captain Hook. "That's my favorite birthday game!"

Shhh, quiet...it is a surprise for Peter!

It's time for the party!
What did everyone bring?

Michael and Cubby
have the chairs.

Shhh, quiet...it is a surprise
for Peter!

HAPPY BIRTHDAY

Wendy hangs banners and garlands in trees. "This will make Peter smile," she says.

Shhh, quiet...it is a surprise for Peter!

Tinker Bell stops, suddenly.
Something is missing. "Presents!"
she says with a laugh. "A little pixie dust
will take care of that."

Shhh, quiet...it is a surprise for Peter!

Shhh, quiet...Peter is coming!
When he arrives, his friends all
shout, "HAPPY BIRTHDAY!"

"Thanks, everybody!" says Peter, happily. "You know what I love best about my birthday? It's that we're all here celebrating together!"